P.I. I LOVE YOU

Miss Demeanor, P.I. Book 1

Joanne Jaytanie

Dedication

I want to dedicate and acknowledge my Go-to-Guy, and husband, Ralph Duncan. He is always willing to answer my questions and help me work through ideas.

Ralph is a licensed professional engineer. He has been accepted into the National Academy of Forensic Engineers and nationally certified as an accident reconstruction specialist. Ralph has provided expert opinions to the legal and insurance industries and consults to numerous law enforcement agencies as to the dynamics and causations of hundreds of accidents. He has testified in both criminal and civil court proceedings. Ralph's training includes, but is not limited to mechanical failures, dynamics, and physics of most types of land, sea, and air vehicles, human factor analysis, human injury biomechanics, and blood spatter analysis.

Table of Contents

CHAPTER ONE

ANOTHER SATURDAY NIGHT. The only excitement in River's life was Bacardi, her homemade mojito mix, and sitting in front of the television with her laptop. Why did she need excitement anyway? It was overrated. She had enough excitement during her eight-hour shifts—at least that's what she told herself. She'd chased down a perp on foot today. Thank goodness for her friends in the *Lady Cops* group. She laughed. "Just because you don't have a life outside work, doesn't mean they don't."

She put her mojito down on the coffee table and stretched out on her sofa. Laptop on her lap desk, she switched it on, sipped on her mojito, and waited for the screen to come to life. She opened her favorites and clicked on *Lady Cops*. Chats were in full swing as she scrolled through to see what was happening.

"Hey, River. What, no hot date tonight?" Maile asked.

"Not hardly. Bear Creek is lacking in the *hot date* department. What about you?"

"I do have a date, with my newly purchased novel, print copy I might add."

"Now that's pitiful—a date with a book." River giggled. "Are Cassie and Shay on-line?"

"Hey, I'm bored. Please, tell me one of you ladies have something juicy to share," Shay said.

"Have you been following the discussion on the shipment of guns intercepted here in Arizona? Not anywhere near me, of course," Cassie said.

"Guns? At least there's action where you live," River said. "We had a herd of mountain goats on Main Street this week—that's what qualifies for action in Bear Creek."

"It's all about your perspective. Mountain goats walking down a street in Prescott, Arizona would be news here." Cassie laughed.

RIVER OPENED A separate message box and sent a private message to the three women.

"About that vacation we've talked about for the last two months: I haven't used any of my days in over a year. What do you say we go for it? Pick out five days and a destination we'd like to visit. Think about it, a chance to chat face-to-face, and experience fun in real life?"

"I'm game," Shay said.

"Me, too," Cassie agreed.

"I'd love to visit Seattle," Maile said. "I realize it's not very far from you, River, if anyone has any other ideas, I'm good with it."

"Far enough. Have I mentioned lately I haven't been out of Bear Creek in forever?" River sighed. "Not even to visit any other places in Montana."

One month later...

RIVER, SHAY, MAILE, and Cassie were relaxing in chaise lounge chairs beside a magnificent infinity pool with a double waterfall. Both were trimmed with Italian tile. The pristine landscaping only added to the ambiance. The view from their chairs encompassed the entire skyline of Seattle, all framed by the Puget Sound. The Sound shimmered like glass on this hot summer day.

"Wow, I never want to leave here," Shay said.

"You're truly certain we aren't going to get a rental bill for this place that will take me the rest of my life to pay off?" Maile asked.

"Absolutely certain," River said as she rubbed suntan lotion over her legs. "Uncle Mike owns this property. He's not really my uncle. Nevertheless, I've known him since the day I was born, and he's always been an uncle to me. He and Dad grew up as neighbors in Portland and remained best friends ever since. Dad asked if Uncle Mike had some place reasonable for us to spend a relaxing week together. Since Uncle Mike's always had properties in Seattle and has always treated me well, he told Dad only the best for his policewoman and her friends would do and insisted this be entirely his treat."

"And I say it again—wow!" Shay exclaimed. "I've never stayed in a place this amazing."

"This place has everything, including a sexy chef," Cassie said. "We don't even have to go out, if we don't want."

"I'd like to spend at least one day sightseeing," Maile said. "I'm happy to go alone, if you girls want to stay here."

"No way. We came here to spend time together. If you want to go sightseeing, I'm in," River said. Cassie and Shay nodded in agreement. "Then let's spend tomorrow at the Pike Place Market and the waterfront. I hear that Pioneer Square is cool, too."

Maile smiled at her friends. "You guys are wonderful. I feel as if we've known each other for years."

"I feel the same way," Cassie said.

"Too bad we don't live closer," River said. "It would be nice to get together for dinner or a movie whenever the mood struck us."

"Wouldn't that be great? How are things going with each of you?" Maile asked.

"About the same for me," Cassie said. "I've closed more cases than my male counterparts and still no talk of promotion."

"I guess I should confess," River said. "It's because of my job I asked you all to get together."

"Why, what happened?" Shay asked.

"One of our officers retired and his position opened up, which should've been a promotion for me. Opportunities like this have only happened two other times in the ten years I've worked for the department and the first time took place right after I got there."

"You didn't get the promotion, did you?" Maile asked.

"No. I've been the top closer for the past two years, but all I got from the captain was a line of bullshit. He said it wasn't my turn. Two other cops deserved it before me. One of them has only been with the department for five years. He's closed fewer cases than anyone else, and *he's* before me?"

"Damn politics." Cassie shook her head.

"Face it. This has nothing to do with politics and everything to do with anatomy," Maile said. "We all work in small towns with small-minded people. We may never work our way up the ladder."

"Ladies, dinner is served." The sexy chef announced and smiled at the women.

AFTER A DAY shopping and sightseeing, the women

were treated to another great dinner cooked by their gorgeous chef. Maile sighed as she joined the others in the living room for after-dinner drinks. She plopped herself down on a buttery soft leather recliner and said, "I love Seattle."

The chef entered with a tray full of golden concoctions adorned with pineapple spears.

"These look luscious, what are they?" Shay asked.

"My specialty, pineapple-mint mojitos," the chef answered.

River's head popped up from her laptop and her three friends laughed.

"Well, at least we now know what will drag you away from that darn thing," Shay chuckled. "We just spent the entire day walking the streets of Seattle, aren't you drained?"

"I was, until I saw this message in my email. How would you ladies like to live in Seattle?" River asked.

"What are you talking about?" Maile asked.

"I'm talking about quitting our dead-end jobs and starting a business of our own, as private investigators."

"What? How?" Cassie asked.

"There's an agency for sale in Pioneer Square. The owners are retiring. We would acquire their client lists and all open cases."

"You're serious?" Maile asked.

"As ever."

"I'd consider it, if I could swing the loan. Except I don't think I could qualify for a business loan and a house loan at the same time," Shay said.

Maile and Cassie agreed.

"I know I couldn't," River said. "But I also know my Uncle Mike would help us out in a heartbeat. Moving back here, only three hours away from my parents and Uncle Mike? He'd be all in."

"You really think so?" Maile asked.

"I do. We wouldn't have a chef or an infinity pool, even so he owns multiple apartment buildings and I'm sure he has a few here. I think we could work out a reasonable monthly rent. I know it's not the same as a house."

"I'm willing to live in an apartment if it means getting our own business off the ground," Cassie said. "If we sell our houses, we could apply the proceeds on the down payment for the business."

"Good point, Cassie. We need to figure out where we stand financially. Between the four of us, we may not need an outrageous loan amount." River tapped her chin with her finger. "I have a thought. There's also another possibility. Investing in businesses is what Uncle Mike does. He may be willing to invest in our business as a silent partner." River paused and looked at each of the women. "If we could show him a reasonable amount of return, I know he'd be interested. We'd also want a buyout option for us down the road. We'd need to work together and develop a business plan."

"I agree. I think if we do this, we need to go through every step as a team. Instead of making River responsible for pitching our plan to Mike, we should go as a united front and give him the entire presentation," Maile said.

"We're a good bet. Each of us has at least ten years' experience on a police force," River said.

"We'll need to do some studying and get licensed as private investigators. I wouldn't think it would be too difficult given our current occupation," Shay said.

"I did a double major in college. My dad insisted I get my business degree, just in case I couldn't get a job in law enforcement. I've also managed my department for weeks when the captain got called away or went on vacation," River said.

"Ironic, wouldn't you say? Your captain picks you to run the department, however he doesn't feel you're qualified for the promotion," Maile said.

"It is all about the anatomy," Cassie reminded them. "We have four more days here. Do you think we can pull this presentation together in that length of time?"

"I'm in," Shay said.

The three women looked at Maile and waited.

"Oh, what the heck. I'm more than ready for a change."

Five months later...

THE FOUR WOMEN stood on the sidewalk outside the massive stone and brick building as workmen expertly handled the lift to hang their sign on a black wrought iron upside-down L-shaped post. They'd placed the post between the two, enormous arched, mullioned windows. In minutes the black rectangular sign with gold leaf raised letters carefully hung, and *Miss Demeanor Private Investigators* became a reality.

June, the owner of the art studio next door, walked out carrying a trayful of filled champagne glasses.

"Congratulations, ladies," said June. "You worked hard to pull this place together in a short span of time. I'm so glad you're here! I feel safer already."

"Thank you," River and her friends said in unison.

"I met Cory, your receptionist, yesterday. She's a lovely girl," June said.

"Actually, Cory is our administrative assistant. She'll hold the fort down and keep the place running," River said.

"Well, enjoy your champagne." June walked back into her studio behind a potential customer.

"I can't believe we pulled this off," Cassie said.

"A new business of our own, and thanks to Mike, affordable apartments on Capitol Hill."

"The best part is we live right next to one another, someone pinch me." Maile laughed. "Ouch!" she exclaimed when Shay did as asked. "I was just kidding," she said as she rubbed her shoulder.

"Well, P.I.s, back to work. Tomorrow is our grand opening. We better get inside and pull this place together," River said.

CHAPTER TWO

T HE ELECTRONIC DOOR chime sounded.

"Good afternoon and welcome to Miss Demeanor Private Investigators," announced a woman with short black hair accentuated with bright blue streaks.

Blake thought her attractive, once he got past the outrageous hair. She was dressed in an extremely short, pleated, blue plaid miniskirt which showed off her long, shapely legs that were clad in shear black tights. Her bright yellow top dipped low, revealing a glimpse of her tantalizing cleavage. One of her ears donned a variety of pierced earrings; the other, only one piercing in the middle of her upper ear that displayed a large deep blue gem. In Seattle, anything was in style.

"Hello," Blake Baxter said.

"How may I help you?"

"I'd like to hire one of your private investigators."

"Certainly. May I ask how you heard about us? Perhaps our flyers, email blast, or our social media page?"

Blake stared at the woman as she rattled through the list.

"Ah, sorry. None of the above."

"Oh, I see." Her spunky attitude faded slightly.

"Don't get me wrong. It sounds like you're doing a great job promoting the business. Would it make you feel better if I told you, someone referred me here?" he asked.

Her sunny smile reignited.

"Yes, I guess I forgot that one," she said as she jotted his name on a piece of paper. "Might I ask who referred you and if you have a particular P.I. in mind?"

"I hear all four women are wonderful, but Mike Dunbar mentioned Ms. Nightingale by name."

"Ah, yes, River Nightingale is one of our primary investigators. She just happens to be in the office.

If you would take a seat, I'll ask if she can see you now." She disappeared into the next room.

The receptionist returned moments later followed by a petite girl. She smiled directly at him, her blue eyes quickly tracking up and down his body. He nearly blushed. As she rounded the counter she held out her hand to him.

"Nice to meet you, Mr. Baxter. I'm River Nightingale. Cory tells me that Mike referred you?"

"Um, he did, except I understood you to be a seasoned policewoman," Blake said. *Geeze, she couldn't be more than nineteen or twenty. Is this a joke?* he wondered.

"Yes. I served in a police department in Montana for ten years and no, I'm not a teenager, I assure you. I happen to be in my mid-thirties."

"I see. I'm sorry for my ill manners."

"No worries, you're not the first person who has thought that and certainly won't be the last. My only hope is when I'm seventy, people will think I'm fifty." She smiled at him again. "If you're still interested in a P.I., I'm sure I can help you."

"Yes, by all means, Ms. Nightingale."

"Then follow me, and please call me River."

She escorted him into the next room. They entered a large open area, with four desks spread throughout. This set-up turned out to be more spacious than he'd thought. It included a conference room that ran along one side of the entire area. Beyond a glass wall he could see a large antique cherry table surrounded by leather chairs. She pulled on the brushed bronze door handle and showed him into the room.

"Before we get started would you like anything to drink? Water, coffee, tea?"

"No, thanks," Blake said.

"What is it I can do for you, Mr. Baxter?"

"Please, call me Blake. My issue is twofold. First, I believe my parents were murdered." He waited for a response from her, but River merely picked up her coffee, sipped, and waited for him to continue. "The police closed the case. They said it was an accident. They believe my father lost control of the vehicle. I don't think that's what happened."

"I see. And your second issue?"

"It's even more complicated. After the death of

our parents, my younger sister, Garnet, and I were going through their personal belongings. My mother kept her own personal safe in her sitting and dressing room. From what the attorney tells me, none of us, including my father, had the combination, only our attorney had it.

"He gave us a sealed envelope with the combination inside. Most of what we found didn't surprise us: her favorite pieces of jewelry, a baby picture of each of us, locks of baby hair. The kinds of things a mother would hold onto. What did surprise us was a sealed envelope addressed to Garnet and me." Blake stopped and rubbed his palms on his slacks.

"Inside was this." He opened his briefcase and pulled out a tiny hospital wristband. He handed the band to River. She held it with great care as she brought it closer to read the faded words.

"Baby girl, Baxter. Calistoga General, California. Your sister's?"

He got the sensation she knew the answer to the question before she even asked it.

"No. We were both born here in Seattle. With the band was a letter that explained what happened.

When I was four and my sister three, Mom admits she and Dad were having problems. I remember that he worked long hours. I believe he likely had an affair. Dad moved out for a while and left the three of us.

"Anyway, I recall a family friend, Mr. George we called him, visiting on a regular basis. A few months later my parents got back together and shortly afterwards, Mom found out she was pregnant. Our mother left and went to visit her parents in Cellar Glen. The only thing I remember was how upset the two of us were that she would leave us behind. She'd never done it before and never did it again."

"And the baby wasn't your father's," River concluded.

"No. Mr. George was the father. We never laid eyes on him after Mom and Dad got back together. Dad refused to allow the child to become part of the family. He gave Mom two choices—the baby or her family. Mom left and went to stay with her parents, in Cellar Glen.

"Calistoga is the closest town with a hospital. She gave birth there to a baby girl, and put her up for adoption. Don't get me wrong. Mom and Dad had a loving marriage as far back as I can recollect, except for this one incident. Garnet and I were their world.

"Anyway, back to the letter. Mom begged Garnet and me to find our half-sister and bring her into the family where she belongs. She mentioned that recently Dad regretted placing Mom in the situation he did. He took full blame for their problems and spoke about trying to locate our sister. He could've found her, if she'd been his priority. But, it seems he died before he could redeem his sins."

"Did your mother arrange the adoption?"

"Yes, a closed adoption. She believed her choice to be the safest for her daughter."

"You're telling me you would like me to investigate your parents' car accident and locate your half-sister? What does your sister, Garnet, think about all this?"

"She's with me one-hundred percent. She couldn't bring herself to come today. My parents' death devastated her. So much so, I've moved back into the family home for the time-being. Garnet moved back home after graduate school. Mom and Dad offered to let her stay until she could save enough money for a down payment on her own place."

"I see. What does your sister do?"

"Like me, she works in the family business, Baxter Imports. We're the largest importer in Seattle. Garnet studied finance and went into the accounting department. My parents were firm believers of working your way up, so she started at an entry level position in the department. Of course, that all changed with their deaths two months ago. Garnet is now chief financial officer and I'm the CEO."

River reached for the pad of paper and pen sitting on the table and made her first note.

"Do you think your promotions caused problems among your employees?"

"No. Everyone knew I would one day take Dad's place and that Garnet would take over Mom's position. My parents started this company together. Mom's family supplied most of the funds to get it off the ground. They were work colleagues who fell in love. Garnet has followed in their path in more ways than one."

"How do you mean?"

"Her boyfriend, Ellis, works in the IT department. Thank goodness for him. He's supported Garnet throughout this experience."

River made another note on her pad.

"Here are all the files and a copy of my mother's letter," Blake said as he pulled out a thick file folder. "The police report of my parents' accident is included. I've notified the detective I would be hiring a private investigator. He definitely came off as less than thrilled when I informed him."

"Is your parents' vehicle still in police impound?"

"Yes. Our attorney sent a registered letter after we received the police report stating the vehicle must not be destroyed until they hear from him."

CHAPTER THREE

RIVER WALKED INTO the precinct on Fourth Street. The building buzzed with activity. She wondered why people weren't falling over one another, given how fast they moved. Yes, she knew cop shops—she'd spent her last ten years living in one, but the little cop shop in Bear Creek, Montana was only slightly larger than this lunchroom she peeked into as she passed by. When she asked for directions to the detectives' bullpen, the sergeant at the front desk looked her up and down, rolled his eyes, then pointed behind him and went back to a pile of paperwork.

She walked slowly by each door, reading the nameplates as she passed, until she came to the door of Homicide Detective Gage Hamlin. The office walls were glass giving her a clear view of the man sitting at his desk studying his computer. His disheveled coffee-colored hair brushed the collar of his button-down royal blue shirt. When he looked over the top of his computer screen, his sapphire-colored eyes locked on hers. River smiled and gave a cursory knock on the half-opened door.

"Detective Hamlin?" River asked.

"Yeah, last time I checked. Do we have an appointment?" Detective Hamlin asked as he grabbed his phone, and scrolled through, looking for an answer.

"No. No appointment. However, if you're not too busy, I wonder if we could chat for a few minutes?"

Detective Hamlin smiled, rose to his feet, walked around his desk, and pulled the door open wider. He gestured for her to enter.

"Sure, I have a few minutes. How can I help you, Miss—?" He grabbed the pile of files and loose papers out of the closest chair and dumped them into the next one over.

"My name is River Nightingale. I'm a private investigator, and I've been hired by the Baxter family to check into their parents' deaths."

River watched as his sparkling eyes and dazzling smile faded from his chiseled features. This reaction would take her a while to get used to. Cops respected other cops, but they had no regard for private detectives. She had firsthand knowledge. Even the cops in her little shop in Bear Creek used to treat them like they were week-old gum stuck to the bottom of their shoes. It irritated her then and it pissed her off now. Although she wasn't going to give Detective Hamlin the satisfaction of knowing how she felt.

"I see," Detective Hamlin said, tight-lipped. "I've no idea why they would hire you. I worked the case and closed it."

"That's the point, Detective Hamlin. The Baxters don't agree with your conclusion and asked me to review your findings."

"Now wait one damn minute. Despite how many open cases are assigned to me, I'm a professional. My work is careful and thorough. On what grounds do they find my work inadequate? And you—you don't even know what kind of hoops I have to jump through. You're just another ambulance chaser, a clueless private dick."

"Sorry to disappoint you, nevertheless I do know what kind of hoops you jump through. I recently left my position as an officer."

"What? Couldn't handle the hard work?" He scoffed.

"I thrive on hard work. I worked hard for ten years and closed more cases than all my colleagues combined. What I do have a problem with is being passed over for promotions while some yahoo, with half the closed cases and experience, gets the job. And why? Merely because he has a dick and I don't."

He made a grunting sound, leaned back in his chair, and crossed his arms over his chest. River stared at him, daring him to make his next nasty comment.

"The case is officially mine, meaning anything you do, anything you discover, you tell me." He popped forward in his chair and started to punch the keys on his keyboard. "Do you want a paper copy, or should I email it to you?" he asked.

She'd let his statement slide for now. They both knew it wasn't true. She didn't need to keep him informed. Even so, no sense ruffling his overly irritated ego.

"My client supplied a paper copy. I would appreciate an electronic one, please." She pulled a business card from her purse and handed it to him.

"Miss Demeanor Private Investigators." Hamlin read out loud. "So, you purchased the old agency."

"That's correct. Along with three friends, who are all experienced policewomen."

"I've never heard your name, and I know most of the cops in the city by face, if not name."

"I'm not from here."

"Huh." He grunted as he studied her.

River quietly withstood his scrutiny. She knew exactly what this jerk was trying to do. He wanted to make her uncomfortable, test her, try to make her fidget or feel insecure. She wouldn't give him the satisfaction.

"I'm heading over to impound right now. Nothing against your report, it's thorough enough. All the same, I'm a hands-on type of person. I find I work better when I'm able to investigate things firsthand and reach my own conclusions. I'll get out of your hair now. I just wanted to stop by, introduce myself, and give you a heads-up about the Baxters hiring me to work their case."

Hamlin simply stared at her. The look on his face—priceless. She couldn't help herself.

Forget not wanting to push his buttons. This man needed a little ruffling. River wanted to smile or stick out her tongue at him. She held her composure. The last thing she needed was to piss him off more. Like he said, the case was technically still his, closed or open, and if she wanted any chance of solving it successfully, it would be easier to have him on her side. She needed to win him over. No better time to start than the present. Her insides cringed and she bit her bottom lip to keep from groaning.

"However, if you're free for a bit, I'd appreciate your insight," she said as she rose from the chair.

"I can't spare you much, but I'll take you over to impound," he grumbled.

HE DROVE IN silence as River studied her file.

No doubt trying to find a screw up, Gage thought. *Well, she wouldn't find a single one.* As with all his cases, he'd made sure he was thorough. Especially with the Baxter case. Shit, the last thing he needed was to muck up the case of one of the richest families in the city, so he'd been particularly careful. Still, he'd make sure to keep a close watch on River Nightingale.

This entire situation came as a complete surprise. Yes, he'd received a call from the Baxter's attorney, but he had to admit, he thought they were blowing smoke. They'd made noise a couple times before and nothing ever came of it. When he saw this pixie-like girl looking in his office window, the last thing running through his mind was private investigator. She didn't look much more than a teenager to him. Her sparkling gold hair, bright-blue eyes, and dazzling smile were sexy as hell and threw him off his game, but only for a short time. He had to give her credit, she could throw his shit right back at him. His razor-sharp comebacks usually intimidated his adversaries. Not this one.

She volleyed them right back at him. He couldn't help himself, it made him smile.

"Did I miss the punch line?" River asked.

"What—ah, nope. Just thinking about another case is all." *Lame Hamlin, very lame.*

He flashed his badge as he drove into the police impound.

"We walk from here," Gage said as he pulled into the first available parking spot. The mangled SUV was parked in the second row.

"Your report stated a single car accident," River said.

"Yeah. Wade Baxter had been driving all day. They got into Seattle around one in the morning, driving down East Madison. We saw a few broken skid marks that suggested excessive speed and overcompensated steering. There were no other vehicles around at the time of the accident. People nearby heard the crash. The front tires hit the curb and the vehicle flipped. Both occupants were killed instantly."

"You found no other skid marks than the ones up the hill? Nothing continuous?" River asked.

"Nope."

"Don't you think it's strange he overcompensated, and didn't even attempt to brake?"

"When you see as much shit as I've seen, nothing seems strange."

"Did you test the brakes?"

"Of course, we did. What do you take me for, a complete jackass?" Gage asked.

"I don't know you and I've no opinion. I'm only trying to get you to tell me something I didn't see in the file."

"Let me put your mind at ease. I had my guys check to see that all fluids in the vehicle were full."

"Did you have a forensic test done on any of the fluids?" River asked.

"No need. They were full."

River pulled out her phone and punched in a number.

"Hey, it's River. How soon can you get over to the police impound and drain the brake fluid on my client's SUV?" She listened. "Great. I need the results as quickly as you can get them done. I know it's a rush job and it will cost me. Believe me; my client will cover your costs. Thanks."

"Who were you talking to?" Gage asked not being able to help himself.

"A friend," she answered slyly.

So, she wants to play this game, he thought.

"Just tell me to mind my own damn business. Don't insult me with your smartass answers. You're not going to find anything." He snapped.

"I think I hit a nerve. You can dish it out, but you can't take it, very well, can you?" She threw him her sexy smile. "Since, as you say, I'm not going to find anything, this shouldn't be of concern to you. I don't want to keep you any longer. Shall we head back?"

The first thing Gage would do when he got back to his office would be to check out River Nightingale. An itch began between his shoulder blades, and he was sure that itch would migrate south, because this woman was clearly going to be a pain in his ass.

CHAPTER FOUR

"HOMICIDE, GAGE, MAKE it quick," Gage answered his phone.

"Detective Hamlin, it's River Nightingale. This is a courtesy call. The Baxter's attorney will be petitioning the court first thing tomorrow to reopen their case."

"Based on what half-baked notion?"

River could hear the sarcasm dripping from his voice.

"The results from my forensic lab."

"You needed a forensic lab to tell you the SUV had brake fluid?" he asked.

"The lab did a chemical analysis of the brake fluid. You were perfectly correct. The SUV was indeed full of fluid. Unfortunately, it was the wrong type. The brake fluid overheated and the brakes failed. Basically, the fluid turned into steam. This caused the brakes to fail."

"What the fuc—"

River cut him off before he could finish.

"Without testing the fluid, you would've never discovered this problem. You see, once the brakes cool, the fluid condenses and appears normal."

"And you know this how?" The heat level rose with each word.

"Personal experience, if you must know. A few years ago, I drove one of the Crown Vics from my department. The brakes failed and I ended up in a corn field. Forensics discovered the brake fluid to be at fault, exactly like the Baxters' accident, repeated heavy braking. Only in my case, it happened during a chase. The ongoing braking led to unexpected brake failure. Ironic, isn't it? The little town of Bear Creek uses a forensic lab. Maybe that's something you should add to your bag of tools. Good night, Detective Hamlin."

River smiled as she hung up the phone in the middle of his extremely colorful tirade. She needed to keep her guard up around this guy. He was smart, quick-witted, and sexy as all get-out. The type of guy who liked to have a good time. The type of guy she'd always seemed attracted to. The type of guy who always broke her heart. Not this time. This time, the only relationship she'd have with sexy Detective Hamlin, was a working one.

"RIVER, THERE'S A Detective Gage Hamlin here to see you," Cory spoke into the phone.

"Does he look pissed?"

"Since I've never met the man, I couldn't say for sure. I can tell you this, he's ultra-hot."

"Thanks, Cory, that's just what I need. You stroking his ego."

"Believe me, I can think of other things to—"

"You finish your sentence and you're fired. I'll be right up."

River heard Cory giggle as she hung up the phone.

"Good morning, Detective. I'm surprised to see you're here," River said as she entered the reception area.

"Thanks for seeing me. Nice place," Hamlin said.

She walked him back to the conference room.

"What's on your mind? Might it have something to do with the homicide?" she asked.

"You know damn well…sorry. Let me start again. We got the petition a few days ago. I've gotten petitions before, only I knew they didn't have a leg to stand on. It's been years since I've been on the losing side. To say my captain reamed me a new one, is an understatement."

"We all make mistakes. We're only human, after all. Cream?" She held out the mug full of coffee she'd poured him while getting her own. He shook his head and took the offered cup.

"Yeah, yeah. Of all the—crap—the Baxter case. Of all cases, this isn't going to go away quietly. You know, basing your case on the wrong fluid in the brakes, doesn't necessarily mean homicide."

"Technically, you're correct. Let me rephrase. This formulation is no longer used in vehicles. Therefore, if it was put into the Baxter's SUV by mistake, it's manslaughter, and if done so on purpose, homicide."

"Who do you think would want them dead?" Gage asked. "Their two children inherited everything."

"And why would their children kill them? They both had everything they needed. They knew they would one day own the company. Why run the risk of getting caught?" River asked.

"Good question," Gage said as he blew on his coffee.

"I don't believe either of the children murdered them. If the kids killed their parents, why would they ask me to investigate their deaths? It makes no sense. They were home free."

"I know. You're right. Just wanted your take on it. Now that the case is reopened, I'll be searching for the murderer. I suppose Blake and Garnet won't need your services any longer."

"Then you would be wrong. I'm still being retained by them."

"They still don't trust us to figure it out?" Hamlin asked. "I guess I can understand their feelings.

Do you have any theories?"

"Now, Detective Hamlin. You know I work for the Baxters, not the Seattle PD." She flashed him a quick smile.

"I thought you might like to cooperate, that's all." Hamlin got up from the chair. "I won't take up any more of your time. If you need me, you know where to find me. Thanks for the coffee."

"I'm sure we'll be seeing more of each other."

Detective Hamlin smiled and gave Cassie a slight nod as they passed one another.

"Who's the hunk?" Cassie asked.

"Down girl. It's Detective Hamlin," River said as she crossed her arms and leaned against the door jamb of the conference room.

"Hm. In all your conversations about him, you failed to mention how smokin' hot the man is," Cassie said.

"True. Except he's also got an ego the size of Texas."

"You on your way out?"

"Yes, I've an appointment at Baxter Imports."

"Darn it. I hoped we could go to lunch. Shay

and Maile are both tied up."

"Let's try and all get together for dinner one night this week. Gotta go."

"RIVER, SORRY TO keep you waiting." Blake greeted her in the waiting room directly outside his office. "I can hardly keep up with the calls. Everyone has heard Mom and Dad's case has been reopened."

"You're not giving out any details, correct?"

"No. You told me not to. I'm very vague in my explanation about new information coming to light."

"And Garnet?"

"I explained it to her and told her not to tell *anyone* what you discovered. I know you want to get a feel for the company and meet as many people as possible. I decided the best way would be a tour, so we'll go through the place, department by department."

Two hours later Blake and River headed for their last stop, the finance department, to meet everyone Garnet worked with on a daily basis. River was disappointed not to find Ellis in the IT Department. She wanted to get an initial impression of the man in Garnet's life.

Blake greeted each employee by name as they walked through the department on their way to Garnet's office. When they reached her door, Blake knocked twice and opened it without waiting for a response. River got her wish. Garnet was wrapped in the embrace of a tall man. They separated as the door opened.

"Blake, your timing is perfect," Garnet said.

River immediately noticed the huge smile on Garnet's face.

"Look." She held out her left hand, showing off a sparkling diamond ring.

Blake flashed a disapproving look, which he immediately disguised with a smile.

"You're engaged? When did this happen?" Blake asked.

"Ellis just proposed to me. Isn't it wonderful?"

"A little unusual. I don't see your office as a romantic setting."

Interesting, River thought. She didn't think Blake appeared too thrilled with Garnet's choice of men, despite his past comments.

"I know, you're right," Ellis said. "I planned on waiting until this weekend and taking Garnet out for a wonderful evening. She's been so upset over the past two months, and now with the reopening of your parents' case, I thought a positive influence would help her cope. Blake, Garnet told me you believe your parents' accident could be a homicide. That is a cruel blow for anyone."

Blake glared at his sister. River stood quietly soaking in the interaction.

"Garnet, you were not to tell *anyone*."

"I know. I haven't told anyone else. I assumed you couldn't possibly mean Ellis."

"What part of *no one* confused you?"

River could see anger and betrayal on Blake's features.

"I've been looking forward to meeting you, El-lis," she said as she stepped forward.

"And you are?" he asked.

"Oh, I'm sorry. I assumed Garnet would've

P.I. I LOVE YOU

informed you about me. My name is River Nightingale."

"Yes, yes she did. I'm a bit surprised to see you here in the offices." His voice was thick with annoyance.

"And why would that be?" Blake asked.

"I wouldn't think you would want your employees knowing about your private investigator."

"Then you would be incorrect. It's because of my private investigator that our parents' case has been reopened."

Blake turned directly to his sister.

"Don't forget about tonight. River is joining us for dinner at the house."

"Oh, I nearly forgot. Well, I'm sure Ellis is welcome to join us," Garnet said as she reached out and took Ellis' hand.

"No, Garnet. Only family."

"I'll be family soon enough," Ellis said.

"And then you will be welcome to attend all family dinners."

Chapter Five

"WHAT'S THE URGENT rush, Garnet? You have your entire life ahead of you," Blake said.

"We don't plan on getting married tomorrow," Garnet said. "It's nice to be able to count on unconditional support from someone."

"What in heaven's name does that mean? I've been your support since the day you were born."

"I know. You're my brother, that's different."

"What do you mean?" Blake studied his sister. "My support's not good enough?"

"That's not what I meant. Stop putting words in my mouth, Blake. I just want Ellis to move in with me. We won't get married until the case is settled, I promise."

"I don't understand why you are in such a damn

big rush."

"Ellis made a good point. If he's here with me, you can return to your place and move on with your own life."

"This entire *moving in* thing is Ellis's idea? Right?"

"I didn't say—"

"Tell me it wasn't," Blake said challenging his sister's decision.

"Okay, he mentioned it first." Garnet raised her hand to stop Blake from arguing. "However, I'd been thinking about it."

"Like hell you have. And you can forget about me moving out. I'm here to stay until this whole mess is over."

Blake's and Garnet's voices echoed through the foyer as their butler led River to the formal living room.

"Sir, your guest is here," the butler announced. "Shall I ask her to wait in the study?"

"No need," Blake said as he walked over to greet River. "Sorry, you caught us at a bad time. We seem to be having more of those lately."

His eyes tracked back to his sister. She blushed and looked away.

"Don't think another thing of it," River said and smiled at her clients. "You're both dealing with a tremendous amount of stress and uncertainty. It's only natural to let it out in the confines of your own home."

"Which is yet another reason Ellis shouldn't move in," Blake said to his sister, and then refocused on River. "Will you join us for a drink?"

AN HOUR LATER the three sat at one end of the largest dining room table River had ever seen. The table was solid Redheart wood and the streaks and patterns were exquisite. She had fallen in love with this wood years ago. She knew from experience that Redheart was an exotic and an extremely expensive wood. River lovingly ran her hand over the table as they chatted about her days in Montana and her decision to move to Seattle and become a private investigator.

"What do you think about Ellis moving in with me, River?" Garnet asked.

"The more people who know a secret, the more likely it will no longer be a secret. Nothing against Ellis, or anyone else, it's just a matter of human nature. You want me to locate your half-sister. It's going to be more difficult to discuss updates if Ellis is living here."

"Ellis is a good man. He's my fiancé. He's not going to say anything to anyone."

"You haven't told him, have you?" Blake asked.

"Not about our sister, no. But the house is large. He could stay in another part of the house when we discuss her."

"This is between the two of you," River said.

"Let's drop it for now, please," Blake said.

Garnet shrugged her shoulders and picked up her water glass.

"Have you found anything more in your mother's belongings?" River asked.

"Nothing more than what we found in her safe. I went through Dad's home office and their bedroom. I found nothing there either," Blake said.

"Do you have any idea who might have wanted your parents' dead?"

They both shook their heads.

"How about people either of them had disagreements with? I'm speaking both professionally and personally."

"Of course, they had disagreements. It's part of life," Garnet said.

"Let's do this. Let's get a sheet of paper for each of you and without discussing it make a list. I'm not saying it's a list of people who might've caused them harm. It's a place for me to start," River said. "Also include how they knew your parents and why they may have disagreed with them."

They left the dining room and Blake led them into what he called the study. River would've used another term, such as the main library in Bear Creek. The siblings sat at opposite ends of the room, while River entertained herself with the unbelievable collection of first editions, including authors like Beatrix Potter, Edgar Allan Poe, and H.G. Wells.

When they both finished their lists, she took them and placed them inside her purse.

"Thank you both for all your input and the wonderful dinner. It's getting late and I've a very busy day tomorrow," River said.

Garnet said goodbye and headed to the stairs. Blake walked River to the door.

"I'll keep you updated," River said.

If it's before ten when you finally finish your work day, swing by my place. We're all here having a drink, not the same without you. Love, Shay.

River pulled the note from her door, walked down two doors and knocked.

"Yes, you made it," Maile said and threw her arms around her friend as if she hadn't seen her this very morning.

Cassie lounged on the sofa and Shay poured a glass of red wine.

"Geeze, girl. We started this business to be in one another's lives, among other things," Shay said as she handed River a glass. "Seems like now, we only see each other's backs."

"And we should consider ourselves extremely

fortunate," River responded with a wink. "Think about it. We've moved to a new city, changed careers, and started a new business that will be in the black before the year has ended."

"I know. You're right. But O.M.G., being successful is sure tiring," Shay said.

"And, here's to being eternally tired." Maile held out her glass.

The four of them clinked their glasses together.

"I suggested to the girls that we should probably set a weekly Monday meeting now that we are picking up speed. It'll give us a chance to check in with everyone and keep Cory up-to-date," Cassie offered.

"I think that's a great idea." River agreed. "Emails are fine, nevertheless meeting in person is better. Tomorrow's Friday. I'll make sure to tell Cory to get it on her schedule. Is eight good? Gives us an hour before our doors open."

"Okay, but we want to hear about your case right now, River. What's with the hunk who wandered through our agency the other day? Is he single?" Shay asked, nearly choking on her laughter.

"If you're referring to Detective Hamlin, I have no idea. We definitely rub one another the wrong way."

"Sounds like the beginning of a wonderful relationship," Maile giggled.

"Yeah, right. Only if he never opens his mouth."

"Tell us about your case, what's going on?" Cassie asked. "It's certainly bringing us some attention."

"This is not your average case. It's genuinely peaked my investigative instincts and kept me on my game." River told them about the Baxters, their accident, and how she had a feeling the first time she saw the car what might've taken place. "Their attorney has petitioned the court and the case is reopened."

"Ouch, no wonder you and Detective Hunk are like oil and water. You stomped all over his little ego," Maile teased.

"Are Blake and Garnet keeping you on to find their parents' murderer?" Shay asked.

"Yes, only that's not even the best part. Trudy and Wade, their mother and father, kept a family secret from them." She explained about the note found in their mother's safe.

"How awful," Maile said. "I don't understand how she could stay in a relationship with a man who wouldn't accept her child."

"Love, pain, guilt. I can't say, and I certainly can't judge. I've given it much thought over the past week. If I were put in the same position, I don't know what I would've done. I'd like to think I'd take all three of my children and leave."

The room went quiet as a cemetery. All four of the women stared into their glasses and contemplated life's twists and turns. Shay rose from her chair, picked up the newly opened wine bottle, and topped off their glasses.

"What's your next step?" she asked.

"I had Blake and Garnet each make up a list for me of everyone they knew who'd ever crossed either parent. Thought I'd start researching each person on their lists in the morning. I'll most likely be in the office all day."

"What about the half-sister?" Maile asked.

"I'm going to start digging into her tomorrow, too," River said as she kicked off her shoes and snuggled into her chair. "As far as potential murderers, there's no real suspects yet. A couple of employees sparked my interest. And then there's Garnet's fiancé, who proposed to her in her office this afternoon. Blake and I walked in on them."

"What? If my boyfriend proposed to me in my office that would be the end of him! Really! Cheap jerk," Maile said.

All four of the women broke out in laughter. They chatted and laughed for another hour, as comfortable around each other as lifelong friends.

"Well, ladies, I hate to do this, but if I don't get at least seven hours beauty sleep, I'm worthless the next day," River said.

RIVER STOOD IN line at the Starbucks one block up from Miss Demeanor Private Investigators. She needed a venti caramel latte if she wanted to make it through her research today.

"Good morning." A deep sexy voice purred in her ear.

She spun around and looked directly into a charcoal-grey tee-shirt. This wasn't any old ten-dollar cotton tee. It fit its owner's well-defined pectorals like a second skin and looked as if it were made of cashmere, sophisticated and stylish without trying.

River balled her hands into fists to keep from reaching up and skimming her palms down the shirt and its occupant. Her gaze glided past the pecs to the vee in the shirt and up into the enchanting indigo depths of Gage's stare. He quirked one side of his mouth. Today he wore a well-groomed beard and moustache. Man, her friends were spot on. This guy was sizzling hot.

"Good morning. Undercover work?" she asked as she focused on his beard.

"Good guess."

He winked at her, actually winked! *Dammit, focus, River; remember your promise. Business relationship...business,* she chided herself.

"Are you stalking me?"

"I was on my way to your office when I saw you cross the street. Technically, I don't believe it qualifies as stalking."

"You do realize we don't open for another hour."

"I know. I have to go back out on my case, and I hoped if I played nice, you would see me early." He attempted to ingratiate himself with a flashy smile.

"I know that look. You want something." She scowled at him.

"What can I get you?" the barista asked.

River rattled off her drink.

"Anything else?"

"I'd like a venti black coffee. My treat," Hamlin said and winked at her again.

"Now I know you want something." She squinted at him and tried for her best *serious look*.

They got their drinks and strolled toward the agency.

"I'm hoping we can share information," he said.

"We're not on the same side. I work for my client, not for SPD, Detective Hamlin."

"I KNOW WHO you work for. I'm not an idiot," Gage snapped.

River wrinkled her nose and rolled her eyes.

This woman could drive him to drink. If he spouted out the first thought popping into his brain, she'd probably smack him upside the head. He counted to five in his mind, before he answered. Feeling a little more in control he continued.

"I realize you don't believe me when I tell you, we *are* on the same side. We both want justice for the deaths of Wade and Trudy Baxter. And, for the love of all that's good, would you *please* call me, Gage."

"I know what'll happen. This information sharing will be a one-way deal, and the recipient will be you."

"No, it won't. I'm more than willing to work with you. My butt is on the line here. I need to find the bastard who murdered them and throw his sorry ass behind bars."

They stood outside the agency.

"You're not feeding me a line of bull, are you?" River glared at him. "Because if you are, I'll make you sorry you crossed me—Gage."

"I believe you would."

"Let me give it some thought."

"Are you busy at seven tonight?" Gage checked the time on his phone.

"I'll probably still be here doing research."

"I'll stop by and pick you up. There's a great grill down on the water. See you then."

HE WALKED AWAY and left her standing there.

Had he just asked her on a date? He did insist she call him, Gage. Don't be silly, she knew all he wanted was to pump her for information. She shook her head and walked into the agency.

"Good morning, boss," Cory greeted her. "What a nice way to start the day, having coffee with Detective Beefcake."

"We were discussing the case. He's trying to pump me for information is all."

"Naw, you're too cute. I say he wants to pump you, period."

"Ha-ha," River responded as Cory's eyes ran with tears of laughter. "I'm so thrilled to be fodder for everyone's morning. Let's talk business, shall we?" She waited for Cory to get a grip on her emotions. "We're going to hold a weekly meeting on Monday mornings starting next week. We'll need you here by eight. We're hoping a weekly meeting will keep everyone better informed."

CHAPTER SIX

RIVER SPENT THE morning checking out every person Blake and Garnet had on their lists. They had a few names in common, although the interesting part was most of each list had totally different subjects. It wasn't unusual. She learned in her years on the force, if you asked ten people what they saw, you would get ten different answers. Throw in genders, and the sky was the limit. Men and women looked at people and situations in completely different ways.

By checking out social media pages, River got a basic overview of each person. She wanted to narrow her list down to six or seven names who jumped out at her. She'd do more in-depth research on each of them. If she came up empty, she'd start over with a new list of possibilities.

GAGE TRIED THE door and found it locked. She'd probably stood him up, he thought. He couldn't blame her if she had. So far, all he'd shown her was his dickhead side. Frankly, it surprised him she'd agreed to dinner in the first place. He knocked and waited. A few seconds later, River walked into the reception area. She unlocked the door and let him in.

"I'm not late, am I? Are you here alone?" he asked.

"The place tends to empty out quickly on Friday nights. The girls asked me to join them for a quick bite to eat and a movie. I told them I still had too much research to get through and needed to put in a few more hours."

He noticed she hadn't mentioned him to her friends.

"I thought it smarter to lock the door, since I can't see it from the back room," she said.

"You need to install a security camera," Gage said.

"It's on our list."

"You mean to tell me the past owners had no security cameras?"

"Seems they were old school, trusted everyone, had no cameras, and no system. We've installed a security alarm. To stay within our budget it was a priority, so our insurance would be affordable. Come on back while I get my stuff together."

"Here, let me help you," he said as she grabbed her laptop, purse, and overflowing briefcase.

"The grill is a few blocks away, I planned on walking. Why don't we leave all your stuff behind the reception desk and pick it up on the way back? I'll walk you home afterward."

"That's not necessary. I can get home."

"This may be difficult for you to believe, given my past performances, but my dad raised me to be a gentleman. There are times I attempt to practice those qualities."

River gave Gage a quick sideways glance and smirked. He could tell she was dying to make a comment. Instead, she stacked her things behind the desk, except for a single file that she tucked under her arm. She dug through her purse, pulled out her keys, and headed to the door. They walked down to the water, past the ferry dock, and continued down Alaskan Way.

"This is the place," Gage said as he pulled the door open for her.

"I've never noticed this place before."

"It's one of the myriads of hole-in-the-wall eateries unique to this city."

They were seated at a table in front of the window with a spectacular view of the Puget Sound. The waiter brought them water and a bottle of wine.

"I'm more infatuated with the city every day." River gazed out the window.

"I know what you mean, I wouldn't live anyplace else, and I've lived in a number of places."

"Where are you from?"

"Don't I feel like a heel?"

"What do you mean?" She frowned and blinked at him.

"I did an internet search on you. I thought for sure you'd do the same."

"I guess I should be flattered."

"Since you didn't, I'm an open book. Born right here in Seattle. I left when I turned eighteen to join the Navy and see the world. You know the old itch—I'm bored, and much too smart to stay in the same city I grew up in."

"And yet you returned?"

He shrugged his shoulders. "What can I say, I wouldn't live anywhere else."

"What did you do in the Navy?"

"I flew fighter jets, the one thing I do miss. Still, I get in the cockpit a few times each year. I put in ten years and decided it was time to come home. I'd wanted to be a cop for as long as I could remember. Yep, typical boy, pilot and cop. Guess there's still time to become a firefighter should the urge arise."

He noticed River relax. She sat back in her chair and picked up her wine. All the while her eyes danced with what looked to him like enjoyment. He took in a slow breath and sat back. He needed to keep his wits about him around this woman. She was bewitching. A man could fall into those depthless, deep blue of her eyes and never be heard from again.

"My turn," he said. "You grew up in Oregon. You went to college, majored in Criminal Justice and Psychology, and moved to Bear Creek, Montana, to serve on their police department. I don't mean to offend you, but why Montana? It's too cold in the winters, and too hot in the summers."

"It's also a breathtaking place. I enjoyed Montana and got to see most of the state. I took the job because they were the first to offer me a position. I wanted to secure a job on my own. I thought a small town would be a good place to start, and in a lot of ways, it turned out, I was right. Much to my dismay, the cowboys in Montana aren't just on the open ranges. They also carry handguns and drive police cruisers. However, no matter how much I outperformed my male counterparts, I would never be promoted above them."

"Why didn't you transfer to another department, or another state?"

"I'd thought about moving. My goal was to make detective. My friends and I met here and spent a week together. While we were here, I saw the ad regarding the sale of the agency. Something clicked inside me. I wanted to become a private investigator. Fight crime and be my own boss. The perfect combination. So I studied and got my license. Believe me, it has some drawbacks. I don't have all the avenues for information at my fingertips, like I did when I was a cop. Even so, I love what I'm doing, except for one thing."

"What might that be?" Gage asked.

"The less-than-pleased looks I get from cops when I tell them what I do." Her eyelids squinted into tiny slits.

"Guilty…sorry about my initial attitude. In case you didn't pick up on it, I'm trying to redeem myself." He waggled one eyebrow.

"I see. I think I'll choose to believe you're being sincere, until you prove me wrong."

Gage feigned offense. He dropped his jaw and gave a little twitch of his shoulders and head. "Well, Ms. Nightingale, I believe you just insulted me."

"No, not at all. Like any good investigator, I can only base my deductions on past performance." She gave him a sassy smile. "Are you going to tell me why you invited me to dinner?"

"You mean for reasons other than your tantalizing personality?"

She nearly choked on the wine as a full belly laugh erupted from her. The sound was so pure and joyful, he couldn't help himself, he joined in—even though he was sincerely shocked at his own reaction. Once the two of them could breathe again, he broached the subject.

"I'm going out on a limb here, but I believe you already have a good idea of who our murderer might be," he said.

"Let me guess. You've way too many suspects and little time," she said.

"Yeah, that about sums it up. Like I said before, we both want the same thing. Does it matter more to you to solve the homicide on your own, or make damn sure the dickwad gets to see the inside of a prison? I mean after all, you've already managed to hand me my balls."

"Detective Hamlin, is that your way of apologizing?"

"Am I more likely to get your help if I say yes?"

She pulled the file from beside her.

"I'm not going to regret this, am I." It wasn't a question. It was a demand. "We're going to share information regarding this case. And…when I come to you with a request, you *are* going to help me."

He saw the fire in her eyes. He believed this was the beginning of a wonderful relationship.

"On that you have my word."

She opened the file and handed him copies of the two lists.

"There are a couple of the same names, but most of the names are different," he said.

She explained to him where she got the lists, and showed him her list of five possibilities.

"Based on the two lists, these are your best guesses?"

"Yes, with one addition. Ellis."

"The boyfriend?"

"Not any more. As of yesterday afternoon, in the middle of the workday, and the middle of Garnet's office, he proposed."

"What the hell?"

"His attempt to comfort and support her—or so he and Garnet insist."

"This is a great start. I'll dig in deeper and see what falls out," Gage said glancing down at the two lists.

"Good. It will free me up for a few days to work on another case I've had to put on the back burner."

"Anything I can help you with?"

"I highly doubt it. Not unless your reach goes clear out to Cellar Glen?"

"A little bedroom community, about forty minutes outside of San Francisco?"

"Yes."

"Well…it just so happens I'm taking a plane to San Francisco tomorrow."

"Really." She looked completely disinterested.

"No, you don't understand. I'm flying a private jet there. Want to join me?"

She squinted her gorgeous eyes at him. "How is it you can afford to own your own jet?"

"I didn't say I owned it. I said I was flying it. A Navy buddy of mine owns a charter company. We trade favors. You're welcome to join me."

"Why are you going to San Francisco?"

"My baby brother lives in the city. We haven't

had a chance to see each other in months. Tomorrow is his birthday. I bought tickets for the Giants game. Good ones, right behind first base. I told him I want to come spend the day with him. He's going to be in seventh heaven when he gets a load of these babies."

"What a nice thing to do. Thank you. Yes, I would truly appreciate joining you."

Gage rose from his chair and pulled out River's.

She stood up and stared at him.

"What, do I have spinach between my teeth?" he asked, a frown creasing his face.

"No. Let's get this straight. I didn't ask for this favor. You offered it. You still owe me."

He leaned in closer, as if to say something he didn't want anyone to overhear. She stood her ground, just like he knew she would. In one fluid gesture, he placed a quick kiss on her silky-smooth lips. River's eyes grew wide and she attempted to step back. Instead she bumped into the table. Gage reached out to balance her.

"Thank you for a productive evening, in more ways than one," he said.

CHAPTER SEVEN

A EUPHORIC SENSATION filled River as they glided along the tops of the fluffy white clouds. Gage expertly piloted the jet. The entire experience was incredible. Especially since she'd never flown in a small plane, let alone a private jet, and sitting in the co-pilot seat, no less.

"What do you think?" Gage asked.

"This is simply amazing. I understand what draws you in. I feel like everything is right with the world and no one can touch me. I feel invincible."

"I'm glad I could introduce you to a whole new world. Once we go back down to earth, did you arrange for transportation?" he asked.

"Yes, there'll be a rental waiting for me when we touchdown. What time should I meet you back at the airport?"

"How about seven? We can meet at the airport café; grab a bite to eat, and then head for home."

RIVER PLUGGED THE directions to Cellar Glen into the car's GPS. According to the GPS, she should be there in about an hour. At this point, all she really knew was the town was small, a population of approximately six-thousand-three-hundred, and most likely, twenty-seven years ago, the population was even less.

Doing research on Cellar Glen had been an arduous task. There was very little information online. From what River had discovered, it appeared the town had finally joined the computer age, but they'd yet to put any historical records online. She'd reached the conclusion that the best option to form a clear picture of the town and its history was to do it the old-fashioned way; visit the county courthouse and search their files. Thankfully, the courthouse was in town and that would save time. She wanted to get a feel for the town, chat with some of the locals, and pay Mrs. Darnell a quick visit.

The Darnells were a very well-to-do family, the first to move into Cellar Glen and commute to San Francisco for work. Mr. Darnell was the founder and owner of Darnell Enterprises, a leading import and export company. Seemed this business ran in the Darnell family. River wondered how much support, other than money, Trudy's father had given to the start-up of Trudy and Wade's company.

She walked into the courthouse and was instantly greeted by a friendly woman.

"Good morning, Miss. You must be new to town. How may I help you?" the woman asked.

"Good morning. My name's River Nightingale, and I'd like to do some research. I'm looking for the list of births and deaths in Cellar Glen for the past twenty-seven years."

"I see. Looking for anyone in particular?"

"I'm here on my client's behalf, and I'm sorry, it's confidential."

The woman studied her for a minute. She hoped the woman wouldn't decide to shut her down.

"I'm not here to make any trouble, I promise."

"Oh, all right. You look like a nice enough young woman. Follow me and I'll show you to our microfiche room."

Uggggh. Her worst nightmare—microfiche. These people really needed to join the current century.

After a couple hours searching, River found what she was looking for, a copy of the town's newspaper for the date that coincided with the birthdate of Blake and Garnet's half-sister. However, it wasn't a list of only the births in Cellar Glen; it included two towns nearby. Now, she had a list of eleven births...four boys and seven girls.

River's stomach growled. She'd eaten breakfast at the crack of dawn. She glanced at her phone and realized it was time to take a break and head to the local diner, get something to eat, and maybe some information. She still needed to locate the Darnell residence. Somehow, they'd managed to keep their physical address from cyberspace, so she'd contacted Blake to get it.

"What'll you have, sweetheart?" asked an older

woman.

"What do you recommend?" River asked.

"Anything on the menu is top-notch. I taught my girls well."

"Oh, you're the owner? It's a very nice place."

"Yep, been in the family since the day it opened. My daughter and granddaughter do all the cooking now. I get to order them around and chat with the diners."

The woman took River's order to the kitchen and returned with her iced tea.

"In town sightseeing?" the older woman asked.

"No, on business. This is my first visit to Cellar Glen. What a quaint, picturesque town. I'm sure I'll return when I can spend more time."

"Sure is, and that's what brought lots of the folks out here to live. Doesn't even bother them, they have to drive over an hour during rush-hour traffic to get into the city."

"Like the Darnells?"

"You know them? They're wonderful folks, and were the first to move here and commute. They're well-off, but never flaunt it. Don't get me wrong, they live in a grand house up on the hill. Anytime you needed help, the Darnells were there."

"They sound wonderful. I don't personally know them; however, I do know their grandkids," River said.

The bell in the kitchen dinged and the older woman walked away. She returned with River's lunch and sat down across from her.

"Ahh," she said. "I love the job, still my old body gets tired faster. It's a real shame about their girl, Trudy. Poor Mrs. Darnell lost her husband a couple years back, and now her daughter. Losing Trudy really hit her hard. It's like she aged ten years in one day. Poor woman." The older woman shook her head.

"I'm sorry to hear that. You think she'll need to move into a home?"

"Never happen. She has no plans to leave. She might've aged physically, but her mind's still sharp as a whip. She always had a housekeeper and a handyman. Until recently, she kept her own gardens. Unfortunately, a couple months back, she needed to hire a gardener. After Trudy's death, she needed a full-time nurse. She turns eighty next month. The town is planning a special party. It's a surprise."

"What a wonderful thing to do."

"Us townsfolk appreciate all the ways the Darnells supported our town. We could always count on them."

"I'm here on behalf of her grandkids. You mind giving me directions to her place?"

"It'd be my pleasure. Before you leave, I want to box up a blueberry pie. Don't get me wrong, her housekeeper is a good cook. But Mrs. Darnell always says I make the best blueberry pie."

RIVER TOOK THE long drive to the top of the hill. The Darnells lived in a mansion, not a house. The gardens overflowed with a plethora of nature's colors. They were expansive and well-kept, as was the beautiful house, from what she could see. She parked her car and walked up and pushed the doorbell.

"Good afternoon," said a handsome middle-aged woman.

"Good afternoon. My name's River Nightingale, and I believe Mrs. Darnell is expecting me."

"She is. Come in. Don't tell me, a blueberry pie?"

"Yes, the owner of the diner wanted me to bring it to her."

The housekeeper took the box.

"Well, this will be a special treat. Mrs. Darnell hasn't felt much like going into town the past few weeks. Maybe this will lift her spirits. Please, follow me. She's in the solarium enjoying the afternoon sun."

Mrs. Darnell sat in a white wrought iron chair with intricate patterns on the back, made more prominent by the pale green cushions attached to the seat and back. She wore well-tailored, ecru colored raw silk slacks, with a matching cream and beige silk top. Her silver hair was pulled loosely back and gathered in a swirl at the base of her skull. A few wisps fell free and framed her elegantly aged face. Her head was tilted back, and her eyes closed, soaking in the rays of the early afternoon. Surrounded by ivies, ferns, ficus, hibiscus, passion flowers, and orchids, River could picture this scene, on the cover of Traditional Home Magazine.

"Good afternoon, Mrs. Darnell. I hope I'm not disturbing you."

"Not at all," Mrs. Darnell said as she leaned her head forward. "River Nightingale, pardon my lack of good manners. I'm not as spry as I used to be. Please, come over and have a seat. I've been looking forward to meeting you."

"Thank you. I too, have been looking forward to meeting you." River took a seat directly across from the older woman.

"I received a phone call from my grandson. He informed me you were working for him, trying to find out who murdered my precious Trudy. Thank you, sincerely, for discovering Trudy and Wade were murdered. Please find out who did this. I will do anything to help you." She reached for the fine lace handkerchief on the table beside her and dabbed her damp eyes. "I attended my daughter's funeral, and yet I feel as though she could walk in at any time." She dabbed again. "How is it I can help you? I didn't know many of their business associates. If my husband were still alive, I'm sure he would be of more help."

"Is that the only thing Blake told you I wanted to speak with you about?"

"Yes," she said in an uncertain tone.

"I came here to speak with you regarding a different subject." River quickly learned people found it extremely difficult to give their loved ones bad news, and would often leave the matter to the police—or private detective.

"I would like to get your take about the accident and anything you may know with regards to the days leading up to it. However, it's not the main reason I'm here."

Mrs. Darnell tilted her head to one side and pursed her lips. "I see."

"I believe this would be easier coming from your daughter." River reached into her oversized purse, which she used as her traveling briefcase, and pulled out a copy of Trudy's letter. River got up, walked over to her, and placed it in her slightly shaking hands. She sat back in the chair and waited for the woman to read the note, deal with the flood of emotions to follow, and finally reach resignation.

"Garnet and Blake know?" the older woman asked as her watery hazel eyes locked onto River's. Tears trickled unchecked down her cheeks. "I begged her, God knows, I begged Trudy not to do this. I tried everything. Told her that her father and I would stand by her side every step of the way, and use everything in our power to make sure she kept *all* her children. She wouldn't do it." Her words came out almost a whisper. "She wouldn't put us, or her children through the embarrassment. She didn't want their lives destroyed by this, as hers turned out to be...I told her she would regret her decision until the day she died. How could I say such a terrible thing to my only child?" She looked at River beseechingly.

"You were her mother. You were trying to keep her from making the biggest mistake of her life. You have *nothing* to feel guilty about. You did everything you could, but the ultimate decision was hers."

"It put a tremendous strain on our relationship with Wade. My husband refused to go visit. Trudy and the children always came here. I only went up when Wade travelled and would be out of town. Please tell me, how are the children dealing with this?"

"That's why I'm here, Mrs. Darnell. Blake and Garnet want their sister in their lives."

River's statement made the older woman cry once again.

"I wasn't sure you would be willing or able to help in this matter. I've researched all I can up to this point. I know seven baby girls were born on the date of your granddaughter's birthday. I can locate each of these women and attempt to narrow down which one it might be. I can direct Blake's attorney to petition the court and open the adoption records. We both know if it was a private, closed adoption, the likelihood of them winning the case is weak, at best."

Sorrow and grief swirled around the older woman. She shook her head slowly, sadly.

"This is exactly like Trudy. She protected her family to the bitter end."

"I don't understand," River said.

"Trudy didn't go through with the adoption, I did."

CHAPTER EIGHT

"THE NURSE PUT the baby girl in Trudy's arms, and she fell apart. Emotionally destroyed, she couldn't function," Mrs. Darnell said as she gazed into space. "She handed the baby to me. Made me promise on my mother's grave I would carry out her wishes, and put the baby up for adoption. She dressed and left the hospital the same day but didn't return home until ten days later. I was beside myself, thinking she'd done something terrible to herself. She went back to her life ten days later, and never spoke of the day again."

Mrs. Darnell shook the letter high in the air.

"Had I known…had I only known Wade talked about locating the girl, everyone's life would've turned out so very, very much differently."

Mrs. Darnell broke down. Her nurse appeared at

her side; the housekeeper close behind. Her soul-deep anguish flowed from the older woman, racking her entire body.

"I think you should go," the nurse said to River.

Darn. She'd come so close to gaining some insight. River nodded and stood. She walked over to Mrs. Darnell, squatted down in front of her, and placed her hands over the woman's.

"I'm so sorry, Mrs. Darnell." With that she rose and headed for the door.

River got into the rental car and dropped her head back against the headrest, emotionally drained. It would be her priority to locate this girl and bring her back to her grandmother. She was startled out of her thoughts by a rap on the window. The housekeeper stood there as River rolled down her window.

"Thank goodness you haven't left," the woman gasped, trying to catch her breath. "Mrs. Darnell is insistent you come back inside. She said her story isn't finished and you need to know the rest."

When River walked back into the house, the housekeeper showed her down the hall and into the library. Mrs. Darnell sat on one end of an antique, high-backed Victorian loveseat, sipping on a steaming cup of tea. When she saw River, she placed the cup and saucer on the coffee table in front of her.

"Thank goodness she caught you." She looked over at the nurse hovering in the corner. "You may go." The nurse hesitated for a moment and then headed for the door. She stopped beside River.

"Please, don't upset her again," the nurse said.

"It wasn't her fault. Please, go," Mrs. Darnell said firmly.

"I'm terribly sorry you saw me in such a state. Seems the sins of our past have come to be heard. Please, sit." She patted the spot beside her.

"There's no need for you to disrupt those six girls' lives. You see, I couldn't bring myself to do what my daughter asked. Trudy's baby girl is her daughter, and my granddaughter. I couldn't send her away to live with people we would never know. I couldn't cut her out of our family. The baby did get legally adopted. There were only four people who knew the truth—me, my husband, a dear friend, who deeply wanted a child and was unable to carry her own to term, and her husband. Tami is a brilliant schoolteacher and she lives in Cellar Glen."

River's jaw dropped. She shook her head as if trying to clear away stars.

"You know where Tami lives?"

"I know where she lives, who she's dating, what her favorite color is, and her deepest thoughts. Her father died over a year ago. Her mother, my friend, is dying of pancreatic cancer. Tami knows me as her mother's best friend. I never told Trudy. In the beginning, I knew if I did, she'd take the baby away, and have an agency place her. As the years went by, I thought if I told Trudy, she would hate me, never trust me again."

This time there were no tears. She appeared to have cried them all out, and what was left behind was her stark heartbreak and regret.

"Wait a minute. You mean to tell me Trudy never ran into your friend and her daughter?" River asked. The puzzlement she was experiencing must've shown on her face.

"I'm sorry. I'm usually much better at explaining. My girlfriend, Tami's adopted mom, and I became friends while my husband and I lived in San Francisco. Tami and her parents lived on the other side of the city. After college graduation, Tami was named Dean of Business at one of the universities. Her mom became weaker and weaker, and Tami drove back and forth every day, from the university to her mom's. She wanted to move her mom away from the city. I suggested they move here and my girlfriend agreed. Tami knows she's adopted. Her parents chose to tell her the truth early on."

"This is more than I could've hoped. Now that I know where Tami lives, after her mom has a chance to explain her story, I can return and speak to her about meeting her sister and brother."

"Let me call Tami's mom and see how she's feeling. Would you mind stepping out for a few minutes?" Mrs. Darnell asked.

"HOW'S YOUR FRIEND feeling?" River asked as she walked back into the library.

"She sounds weak and tired, but she doesn't want to put this off any longer. I think she's afraid she'll die and not get the chance to explain everything to Tami. She told me she'd talk to Tami this weekend. Would you mind if I keep this letter?"

"It's a copy I made for you. Did you tell her about the current situation?"

"Yes, I did. I also told her about the letter. She would like a copy when she broaches the subject with her daughter. I gave her your name and number and asked them to contact you or me."

"A wise idea. I will be sure to keep you in the loop," River said. "Thank you for telling me this. When the time comes, I believe it would be easier on Blake and Garnet for you to be the one to tell them who their sister is. Tell them the same story you told me. It's important for them to know every detail."

Mrs. Darnell reached out and took one of River's hands.

"Thank you so much for coming out today. I feel a great burden has lifted from me. It will be difficult to explain all this to my grandchildren, be that as it may, I believe you are correct."

TWILIGHT FELL BY the time River left Mrs. Darnell's home. She headed out of town, turned on the music, and absently hummed along as her brain clicked into overdrive. You never could tell how complicated or difficult a case would be to solve. She'd thought it would be months, maybe more, until she discovered the identity of the Baxters' half-sister. River had hoped Mrs. Darnell would at least be able to point her in the right direction. She never dreamed she would hear what she'd heard from the older woman. She shook her head at the loss of it all.

For an instant, River was blinded as the headlights behind her filled her rearview mirror. She squinted and glanced into her side view mirror. The vehicle appeared to be approaching quickly. *Someone's late for a hot date*, she thought. She decided her best course of action would be to move closer to the shoulder and slow down, the international sign for inviting a vehicle to pass. As she started her maneuver, the headlights grew brighter. Suddenly the rental got rammed from behind, the momentum snapping her upper body into the seatbelt. Her head missed the steering wheel by a scant inch.

"What the hell," she said and got rewarded with another slam from behind. "Dammit, this guy is serious."

Obviously, a date was not this driver's agenda. She punched her foot down on the gas as her rear window shattered into a million tiny pieces. Another gunshot hit her car and she swerved and ducked. Head low to the steering wheel, she reached out and punched the speed dial button on her phone.

GAGE'S PHONE VIBRATED on the table and lit up with River's picture he'd taken the other night at dinner.

"Don't worry. The flight won't leave without you. Truth be told, you're not late for another fifteen minutes. I'm just hanging out sipping on lemonade. When we touchdown in Seattle, I could use something stronger," he said.

"Gage, someone's shooting at me," River said with a twang of alarm in her tone.

He dropped his feet from the seat across from him and sat up straight.

"Are you positive? Damn, scratch that, ex-cop."

He heard glass breaking in the background.

"Get your gun out, the asshole means business." He demanded.

"I can't. I left it in the trunk with all the rest of my stuff."

"What the hell did you do that for?"

"Because I visited a little old lady, in a village, and didn't expect to be assaulted on my way back."

"Wonderful." He threw a few dollars on the table, grabbed his gear and headed for his car. "Where are you?"

"By my estimation, I'm about fifteen minutes west of you. I'm hoping they'll break off before we get to civilization."

Gage headed out of the parking lot in River's direction.

"Yeah, good luck with that. Keep playing offense. We should meet up in about six minutes. I'll flash my lights as I approach. You keep coming. I'm gonna box him in. And stay on the line."

He heard more glass break and the squeal of her tires as she tried to keep from being an easy target. Then he heard a crash and a grunt from her.

"River?" Adrenaline surged through Gage's system.

"I'm all right. He caught up to me. Shit, here he comes again."

Another sound of crushing metal and her hiss came through his phone.

"You should be seeing my headlights any second, hang on." *Damn, where the hell was she?* he thought. He broke the crest of a small hill and saw a set of headlights weaving, another pair directly behind her car. *Thank God.* He flashed his headlights.

"I see you," River said sounding a little out of breath.

"Keep coming dumbass, you're mine now," Gage said to the assailant, as he flattened the gas pedal to the floorboard.

As if reading his mind, the attacking vehicle broke off to the right, and down a dirt road, leaving a wave of stones flying in every direction. River's car flew by and Gage hit the brake.

"River, he broke off. River?"

"I hear you. I'm slowing down. Let's keep going until we get to the airport."

Gage shook his head. He'd been exceptionally impressed. Not only was this woman witty and attractive, but dayum, she could handle a vehicle.

She pulled into the airport parking area and he pulled up beside her. He jumped out of his car and ran over to her, yanking the driver's door open. She sat there, arms crossed over the wheel and head leaning against them. He knew the feeling, a queasy stomach as the flood of adrenaline tapered off.

"Let me help you out," he said.

He heard her take in a deep breath and sit up. He could see a large bruise starting over one cheek where she'd probably hit the wheel.

"Unhook your belt," he said.

He saw her grimace as she reached for the buckle.

"Ribs?"

"Yeah. I'm certain they're bruised, I might've cracked one or two," she hissed between clenched teeth.

Finally releasing the belt, she slowly turned in

his direction. He saw the blood covering her upper arm and shoulder. It looked like she'd been hit with a bullet or piece of flying glass.

"You're bleeding." He pointed to her shoulder.

"He nailed me on the first shot. It went straight through. I don't think it hit the bone."

She winced as she attempted to use her injured arm to get out of the vehicle. Gage leaned in, slipped an arm under her injured arm and around her body, and then lifted her from the car. She bit her bottom lip, a stifled whimper escaped anyway.

"Can you stand?" he asked.

"I think so. My legs feel like jelly, but I don't think they're injured."

Gage gently set River on her feet. He held on to her until he felt her balance herself.

He scanned the front seat to make sure she'd left nothing and quickly counted six gunshots which had torn through the seat. The nose of a bullet protruded from the seat. Another inch and it would have pierced her spine.

"You said all your things are in the trunk?"

"Yes."

He walked to the rear of the vehicle. The entire

back end smashed nearly to the now-missing back window.

"This doesn't look promising," he said. "They really nailed the back end of this car. Hope the clients you're working for have a lot of money."

"I've got insurance," she said and attempted a smile.

"Ever read the fine print? I don't think it'll cover gunshots; maybe the other damage."

"I'm not worried. Blake won't care."

"Blake? As in Baxter? I thought you were working another case?" he asked as he pried the trunk open.

"You're right, I did say another case. I never said another client."

He pulled her oversized bag from the trunk, placed it on the ground and gathered all the loose papers into a pile. As he did so, he noticed the names Darnell and Tami.

"You're not reading my files, are you?" She'd limped to the back side of the vehicle and stood, all fiery four and a half feet of her. He grinned at the sight.

"Sorry, tried not to. But I have to admit, I caught

a couple words."

"And you will tell no one what you've seen."

He stuffed the papers into the large bag, searched the trunk one last time and caught the shimmer of metal—her gun. He reached into the back of the trunk and picked up her Sig P238. He looked it over. It looked as if it had weathered the beating, but it would need to be taken apart and checked to make sure. He placed it into her bag.

"Geeze, you'll do anything to get out of dinner with me," he said.

She laughed, and then cringed as she drew her good arm around her ribs.

"Sorry about that. We need to get you to a doctor."

"Can you triage me well enough to get us back to Seattle? I'd rather see one there. Besides, that way you don't need to stick around, you can drop me off.

"You're joking, right? There's no way in hell I'm going to leave you at the Emergency door of a hospital like a drive-up coffee stop. Let's get you into the jet and let me take a good look at you in the light."

CHAPTER NINE

"TAKE A SEAT right here. Let me see what I have to work with in the way of first aid supplies," Gage said. He helped her into one of the buttery leather captain's chairs in the main salon of the plane.

He returned with a first aid kit hung around one arm and a carefully balanced pile of items, including a couple bags of ice on top. He dropped everything into the chair beside her.

"Here put this on your cheek," he urged as he handed her one of the ice bags. "First thing we need to do is get this shirt off you, so I can get a look at your arm, shoulder, and ribs." He pulled a pair of scissors from the first aid bag.

"Just one minute," River said. She pulled the ice away from her face and glared at Gage. "I can pull my shirt over my head."

"And pull your ribcage at the same time. It's not like you're going to wear this again, it's soaked in blood, and then there's this." He put two fingers through the holes near the shoulder. "I admit, this isn't the way I pictured getting you naked."

"And what makes you think you'll ever have a chance to get me naked?" She stared at him as her eyebrows furrowed.

He chuckled and tugged at the bottom of her pullover.

"Blast it all. This is my brand-new charmeuse pullover."

He unceremoniously cut his way up the entire length. As he pulled the two pieces away from one another, he had to consciously keep from reacting. The entire side of her ribcage was already turning shades of red and purple. However, it wasn't the reason for his reaction. Her hot pink bra veed low between her perfect breasts, the vee held together by a delicate release. His fingers nearly reached to unhook it. *Come on man, get a grip*, he thought. After all, this wasn't the first time he'd triaged a woman, it was however, the first time a woman affected him this way.

"How does it look?" River eyed him. "Before you answer, I'm talking about my ribcage, not my bra."

"Ummm." He attempted to stall, trying to get the log-sized, sandpaper-covered-thing called his tongue to function. He grabbed one of the bottles of water he'd brought and slugged back a gulp. He put it on the floor beside him, opened the other bottle and handed it to River. He swallowed. "I'd say fifty-fifty you cracked one, but you sure as hell bruised the daylights out of them. Either way, it's gonna be a painful night."

He grabbed the scissors again and sliced through both sleeves, paying extra attention to the one covered in blood.

"Ouch," River said.

"I'm trying to be careful, your shirt is already started to stick to your wound. I'm going to have to clean you up." He stood up. "There's a single bunk in the rear salon. I think it would be better if you lay down."

"Bet you say that to all the girls." River stood up

and immediately began to sway.

"Crap, don't—" He caught her before she hit the floor and landed on her shoulder.

RIVER EXPERIENCED THE sensation of floating on water, riding gentle waves, her mind in a green haze. The first sound she registered was a beeping. She tried to reach for her nightstand to hit the snooze button for just ten more minutes. As she reached out, a searing pain shot up her arm.

"Good, you're awake. You had me worried."

Is that Gage's voice? River wondered, still not fully conscious of her surroundings. *Why on Earth would he be in my bedroom?*

"River. Come on now, nap's over," Gage urged.

She turned her head in the direction of his voice. She opened her eyelids a slit.

"Hey there, sunshine. Good to see those baby blues again." His thumb lightly stroked her hair back from her cheek.

He *was* in her room. Wait, this wasn't *her* room.

She pushed her hands into the bed and attempted to raise herself into a sitting position.

"Ouch!" She couldn't decide which hurt worse, the pain vibrating through her ribcage, or the one shooting up her arm.

"Here, let me help you." Gage picked up the pillows from the end of her bed, helped her lean forward and laid her gingerly against the pillows. His lips brushed her hair.

"How'd I get here? The last thing I remember was giving you a hard time about your so-called triage."

"Hey, now. The doc said I did a great job." Gage flashed her a killer smile. "You don't recall dropping to the floor of the plane?"

She slowly shook her head.

"You didn't actually hit the floor. I caught you just in time. Patched you up, flew back to Seattle, and got you here, into the hospital."

"How's our patient?" asked the doctor as she swept into the room.

"She just woke up, Doc. And, I get the feeling she's not a morning person." Gage chuckled.

"We'll cut her some slack, due to the night she had, and because it's not even dawn yet," the chipper doctor said. "You were one lucky woman, Ms. Nightingale—"

"River, please."

"Okay then, River. You're very lucky your shooter had poor aim and your partner has such good knowledge of medical triage. The bullet passed through your upper arm. A half inch higher, it would've hit your shoulder. A hair closer and it would've gone straight through your humerus. All in all, you had the best possible outcome.

"You need to take it easy and don't pull on your sutures for the next couple weeks. Translation—*no* heavy lifting. You did a real number on your ribs. Much to my surprise, you didn't crack or break them. I'm going to warn you, they will be sore for a few weeks. Be sure to ice your cheeks every few hours for the next day. Ice will help with the swelling and bruising."

"Thank you. When can I go home?" River asked.

"I planned to keep you until at least tonight, just to make sure. However, Gage here has offered to stay with you until tomorrow. I'm holding him responsible for your care." The doctor smiled at Gage and River.

"But, I don't—" River started.

"Yes, you do. You're fortunate you didn't break any bones, or ribs; even so, your body experienced extreme trauma. I'll send you home with something for the pain. No driving while you take these pills, and you're absolutely not to get behind the wheel for the next three days, with or without the pills. Your discharge papers and meds will be here in the next hour or so. Please, for your own well-being, take it easy for at least a few days. You'll heal quicker."

River narrowed her eyes and shifted her gaze in Gage's direction.

"You're welcome. And, by the way—you scared the living shit out of me. So, do me a favor and follow the doctor's directions."

Taken aback by his sincere concern, her anger deflated.

"I haven't said thank you. Thanks for taking care of me and getting me to the hospital. I'm sorry I've inconvenienced you. I'm sure you had better things to do than hang out at a hospital."

He shook his head and scolded her. "What'd you think I would do, drop-kick you to the curb? You've so little faith in me, or is it the male gender in general?"

"I guess my experience with your gender over the years has jaded me. I never used to be this way. I love my dad and can always count on my Uncle Mike. If I really think about it, they are the only two males who've been trustworthy. I've learned to fend for myself."

"Sorry to mess up your standing rule, but I'll be damned if I'll leave you alone. You need someone to look after you, doctor's orders. Besides, I've grown kind of fond of you." His face remained serious.

"What about your cases, your work?"

"Already solved. I told my captain I'm working the case with you."

"I'm a P.I. remember? Cops and P.I.s don't usually play well together."

"Maybe so. Let's start something new, this time we'll work together. I'll get you home and settled.

Then I want to hear all about what you were working on and who was shooting at you."

SHAY, CASSIE, AND Maile burst into River's apartment as Gage gently lowered River down on the sofa.

"River, how are you feeling?" Maile asked, concern etched her features.

Shay nudged her shoulder into Cassie, and the two smiled at each other.

"Looks like she's in good hands," Shay giggled.

"Funny, very funny," River said.

"Nice to meet you in person, Gage," Maile said.

River looked from her three friends to Gage and back.

"We tried to call you late last night when Maile realized you still weren't home. Gage explained what happened," Shay said.

"I'll be fine. Thanks for stopping by. Doctor said all I need is rest."

Gage rolled his eyes.

"I'd be fine too, with a nurse like him." Cassie waggled her eyebrows.

"Don't you women have an agency to open?" River asked.

"Hint taken." Shay poked the other two in their backs.

"Call us, if you need us," Maile said as they left the apartment.

"They seem like great friends," Gage said.

"The best."

River's phone rang. She tried to reach out to pick it up from the coffee table and cringed.

Gage shook his head in disgust as he picked up the phone and handed it to her.

Blake Baxter's name displayed.

"Morning, Blake."

"We have a problem. I walked into the house last night and overheard Ellis and Garnet arguing. Seems Garnet told him about our sister, and Ellis was none too happy. He wants her to leave it alone. Ellis questioned her as to why she would be willing to lose half of her inheritance to a perfect stranger."

"Ellis sounds like a real gem. Let me give this some thought and I'll get back to you later today." Gage frowned at her. "For now, let's keep this between you and me." She disconnected her call and looked Gage squarely in the face. "If the offer is still on the table, I could use your help."

"On two conditions. First, we get some breakfast. I'm starved, and I know you haven't eaten since yesterday."

"And the second?"

"You're going to start at the beginning and tell me the whole sordid story."

CHAPTER TEN

"LET ME GET this straight. You specifically instructed Garnet to keep this between the three of you, and she couldn't keep her mouth shut. Love will make you do stupid things." Gage shook his head.

"If it really is about love, don't you find it strange Ellis's primary concern is over her inheritance?"

"What are you getting at?"

"Obviously, I'm talking about the money."

"Hold on. You think Ellis is in this for the money and he really doesn't love Garnet?"

"From the way I see it, the pieces are fitting together. He's been with her through the entire ordeal of her parents' murder. He's pushing to move into her home. The scumbag proposed to her in her office, for crying out loud."

Gage lifted River's legs up from the sofa and scooted under them, lowering them across his lap. This seemed natural to him. Looking after River triggered a primal need. He had believed when he returned to Seattle he'd come home. How wrong he'd been. River made him whole, happy, kept him on his toes, and drove him crazy. Maybe Seattle was home. However, he knew with no doubt, River was paradise. As though she'd been a part of his life forever. *Shit, is this what love feels like?* He shook his head, forcing himself to refocus his thoughts.

"What do you think?" River asked.

"About what?"

"Were you even listening to me?"

"Sorry…tell me what you said."

She puffed out a breath and gave him a stern look. He could see the wheels moving in her head, trying to decide whether to start an argument or repeat what she'd said.

"I asked if you could borrow your friend's plane again."

"And go where?" If he wasn't confused before,

he certainly was now.

"Back to Cellar Glen. I'll give Mrs. Darnell a call, tell her my plan and see if I can get her to agree to flying back here with you to speak with her grandkids."

"And just when do you plan on us doing this?"

"The day after tomorrow."

"You can't fly then."

"I don't plan to. I'll be putting together the rest of my op."

"First of all, the doctor said no driving for the next three days. It sounds to me like you intend on driving somewhere."

"I do. I'm going to nail the bastard who killed Wade and Trudy Baxter."

"Now I see where you're going with this. You believe Ellis killed the Baxters and had you followed to Cellar Glen."

"Yes, I believe Ellis cleared the way to Garnet's inheritance when he killed—or had someone kill—her parents. Now, he finds out there's a half-sister. Based on my character analysis of him, he will try to find her. Even better, if given the opportunity, he'll stop the one person who might know the sister's identity."

"But Ellis doesn't know that you know who Tami is."

"No, he doesn't. He does know I went to Cellar Glen to visit their grandmother. By any chance, is there anyone you know who could get to Mrs. Darnell as soon as possible and keep an eye on her until she can be picked up?"

"Today is your lucky day." He winked at River. "He won't do it for free."

"I didn't expect he would. Blake will cover the expense. Just get him out there now."

"Let me go make a call."

"While you do that, I'll call Mrs. Darnell."

AFTER HIS CALL, Gage went back into the living room carrying a cup of tea and handed it to River.

"Thank you," she said with a look of surprise. "What did your friend say?"

"He's on his way over there right now. He'll be knocking on her door in fifteen minutes, to introduce himself. Did you fill Mrs. Darnell in on your plan?"

"I did. There's a slight change. Tami's mother explained everything to Tami. She happened to be visiting Mrs. Darnell when I phoned. Tami wants to come along, too."

He thought the plan through and must've frowned while doing so.

"Problem?" she asked.

"Not at all. Just want to keep the players straight. By the way, I'm staying right here in Seattle. I'll be your driver and my friend can fly out and pick up Mrs. Darnell."

"I need to phone Blake and set up a meeting place in a couple hours. Would you mind being my chauffeur?"

"I would be honored, under one condition."

"Geeze, again with the *conditions*. Have you always been this way?"

"If you must know. No…not until the day when a sassy, pixie-like vixen strutted into my office and challenged me at every turn."

She wrinkled her forehead and tilted her head from one side to the other. "Is there a compliment somewhere in there?" River asked.

She looked up at him, her enchanting blue eyes filled with uncertainty. He couldn't help himself. He took the cup from her and set it on the coffee table. He bent toward her and touched her lips with his. They were even softer than the first time he'd kissed her. River's lips felt like pure velvet. She reached up with her uninjured arm and ran her fingers through his hair, pulling him closer to her. Tenderly he placed one hand on the unbruised side of her face and deepened the kiss. The taste of River Nightingale intoxicated him. She'd become his addiction. He slid his hand down to her chin and cupped it. The thought of hurting her tugged at him. Summoning all his willpower he pulled back. River's eyes fluttered open.

"I think I like your *condition*."

"That had nothing to do with my condition," Gage whispered, his lips mere inches from hers. "It was pure need." He closed the distance again with a soft, quick kiss and then he stood up.

"You need to rest. Call Blake, set up a meeting for seven tonight. Meet at a restaurant, someplace where we can talk without the chance of being overheard. After your call, turn off your phone and sleep."

"WHAT'S HE DOING here?" Blake Baxter asked as he stood looking at River and Gage sitting at the table. "And what the hell happened to you? I hope it wasn't due to my case." His anger seemed to abate.

"Gage has agreed to work with me. Take a seat and I'll explain," River said.

"Right. He's done with my parent's case. He claims it was my father's fault," Blake snapped.

River started to defend Gage, but before she could, he placed a hand on her knee and gave it a slight squeeze. She put her hand over his in an unspoken understanding, and he rotated his hand to lace his fingers through River's.

"You've every right to feel the way you do, Blake," Gage said. "At the time, my conclusion was based on the data I had available. I did a thorough job with what I had to work with, and believed my conclusion correct. I'm not sorry for that." Gage watched as Blake bristled and continued. "I am sorry for my incorrect conclusion. And for that, I sincerely apologize and hope you will allow me to set the record straight."

River and Gage waited while Blake digested the information. They watched him, neither making a single move.

"Thank you for your apology," Blake finally said. "I do believe you did your best. We're all human, and we all make mistakes. It takes a special person to admit when they're wrong and I welcome your help."

Gage heard River let out a breath. He'd been holding his too, but hoped no one noticed.

"Great. Let's get started," River said.

"Hold on." Blake held his hand up, to stop River from continuing. "You didn't answer my second question. Are the bruises on your face linked to my case?"

"Yes. I'm getting a little too close for someone's comfort. I suppose I should tell you now. You'll probably receive a large bill from the car rental place," River said.

"You dinged up a car, don't give it another thought."

"She didn't *ding* it," Gage said as River frowned at him. "Some jackass used her as a moving target. Between ramming the back of River's rental and shooting at her, she's damned lucky to be here tonight."

Blake looked at River in horror. "Are you going to be all right? Are you sure you should be here?" His total demeanor changed.

"It's part of my business. I'll be fine, a bit sore is all," she answered.

The waiter came to take their drink orders. Gage ordered River a sparkling water with lime and got yet another dirty look. When the waiter left, River jumped into her plan.

"I'd like you to inform Garnet and Ellis that I want to meet with the three of you tomorrow afternoon to update you on the case. Time and place is up to your discretion."

Blake nearly choked on his sip of water.

"Ellis? Why Ellis? I've argued a number of times

P . I . I L O V E Y O U

with Garnet about keeping family business private."

"And it will be a perfect opportunity to explain yourself," River said. "Tell her you've given it some thought about what you said and you were wrong. Tell Garnet she's correct. Ellis will soon be part of the family and as such should be included."

"If that's what you want," Blake shook his head in disappointment. "And thanks, I'm gonna get a ration of shit from my sister. I still don't understand why you want him there."

"There's a possibility either Garnet or Ellis could be leaking information."

"Well, I can tell you, it's not Garnet. I admit, she doesn't seem able to keep from updating Ellis, but that's all it is. So, that leaves, Ellis. For what purpose would he leak information?" Blake asked.

"Difficult to say," River said. "It could simply be he's relaying the information in general conversation with someone. Tomorrow, I will inform all of you, your grandmother will be coming to town the following day, and she has something she would like to discuss with you in person. Gage and I will pick her up at SeaTac and bring her directly to the house."

"What? Gran's coming here? I'm thrilled…but what could she possibly tell us?" Blake asked. "Tell me, what does she know?"

"She wouldn't tell me. She just asked that I arrange the meeting."

"Is this regarding my parent's homicide, or my half-sister?"

"If we're on the right track, both."

"I COULDN'T HELP but notice you didn't tell him the entire truth," Gage said. He opened the car door for River and helped her in. The meeting had drained her, she was clammy and pale.

"I'm not going to point fingers at his sister's fiancé until I'm certain," River said.

"Hm…I thought it might be because you still aren't sure he won't run back to his sister and tell her everything."

She gave him a sly look and smiled.

CHAPTER ELEVEN

"ROGER," GAGE SAID and hung up his phone. "That was my pilot friend, the flight went as planned. The soft-clothes officers were there upon arrival and took Mrs. Darnell and Tami to the safe house." He informed River.

The two of them along with another cop who was playing the part of a decoy of Mrs. Darnell headed south on I-5.

"Good to know. Have we picked up our tail yet?" River asked.

"Can't say for sure, but our rest stop is coming up soon."

His phone beeped and he glanced at the text displayed.

"They're all set at the rest stop. This should go smoothly."

"From your mouth," River said.

Gage popped on his headlights as the sun set.

"I'm sure glad we waited until after sunset to run this op," Gage said as he glanced in the rear-view mirror. "I mean you're good, but I don't think you could pull off Mrs. Darnell in the daytime."

"You're welcome, numbnuts," replied the female officer in the backseat.

"Oh, I see you two have worked together before." River giggled.

"You could say that." The officer rolled her eyes.

"Funny," Gage said. "Let's get our game faces on. We're two miles out."

They pulled into the rest stop and parked across the lot and a few spaces down from the restrooms. A dark-colored sedan pulled in a few minutes later and parked four spaces away, placing another parked car between them.

Gage and River got out of the car. Gage headed for the restrooms, while River helped Mrs. Darnell from the vehicle. The two women entered the restroom together. Shortly after, Mrs. Darnell exited the restroom and walked back toward their vehicle.

She strolled by their car and walked over to sit at the picnic table directly in front of the dark sedan. Her back was to the sedan.

The passenger door and one of the back doors of the sedan opened. Two men got out and looked around the rest area. There were two other vehicles in the area, the one between them and Mrs. Darnell's ride, and a pickup truck with a horse trailer attached, half-a-dozen spots away.

The two men nodded to each other and headed in the direction of Mrs. Darnell. In less than thirty seconds they taped her mouth, threw a bag over her head and dragged her back to their sedan. One man shoved her into the backseat, and jumped in behind her as the other got into the front.

"Go, go, go…" Came the voice through the radio Gage held in his hand. The pickup backed into the middle of the parking area, and the doors of the horse trailer sprang open, six officers in complete riot gear jumped out, armed with Remington 870 shotguns aimed at the sedan. The sedan started backing up quickly. Sirens blared and lights flashed as police cruisers blocked all exits in and out of the rest-stop. The sedan stopped, but there was no other movement.

Gage took the bullhorn handed to him.

"You're surrounded. Throw your weapons from the vehicle and come out with your hands up. Any hostile actions will be met with deadly force."

Nothing happened. They waited a beat, then two.

"Okay," yelled the driver. "We're tossing our weapons."

The weapons were tossed, and the three doors opened. The three men exited the vehicles hands held high in the air. The policewoman came out directly behind them, her gun drawn and pointed at the two men in front of her.

TWO HOURS LATER, Gage and River headed for the Baxter residence.

"I have to admit, it kinda surprised me those imbeciles gave up as easily as they did," River said.

"Guess they were smart enough to know they wouldn't get out of their predicament in one piece," Gage said. "What surprised me was how fast they flipped on Ellis."

"They didn't want to go down for the murder of the Baxters. Thanks for verifying their stories of being in Hawaii so quickly."

"My pleasure," Gage reached out and covered her hand in his.

"We work well together. I see a productive future for us," she said and smiled at him. "In more ways than one." River laced her fingers in his, brought them up to her mouth, and kissed his hand.

They arrived at the Baxter residence just as a handcuffed Ellis was being escorted to the waiting police cruiser. Blake held his sister, Garnet, as she sobbed into his shoulder.

"I feel sorry for Garnet. Her whole world has crumbled around her," Gage said.

"Better now than after she married the bastard and he killed off the rest of her family and then her," River said.

An unmarked vehicle pulled up and Mrs. Darnell was helped from the back seat. River walked over and greeted the older woman.

"I can't begin to thank you for what you've done

for my family," Mrs. Darnell said.

"They still have some difficult times ahead. But at least their parents' killer will be prosecuted," River said.

The door on the other side of the vehicle opened and a young woman stepped out. She looked like a combination of both Blake and Garnet.

Blake noticed his grandmother and the other woman. He said something to Garnet and pointed in their direction. Garnet wiped her eyes and followed her brother down to the car. He reached his grandmother first and hugged her fiercely, his love for her evident. Garnet followed suit.

"I thought it past time you met your sister, Tami," Mrs. Darnell said.

Time seemed to crawl by as the three siblings gawked at one another. Shock and surprise flashed across both Blake's and Garnet's faces. Finally, Garnet smiled and wrapped her sister in a bear hug, tears streaming down both cheeks.

"My baby sister!" Garnet said as she pulled away only far enough to look at Tami and then hugged her again. "Welcome to the family. I feel as if I've known you my entire life. We've a lifetime of catching up to do. Both of us want to hear all about your life. Everything. The important events and the everyday happenings."

Tears welled up in Tami's eyes and started to leak. Garnet pulled away, still holding her shoulders as she studied the girl.

"I can't wait to show you pictures of Mom at your age. You look just like her, doesn't she, Blake?"

"She does, yes," Blake said.

"Thank you, very much for welcoming me. I had no idea what your reactions would be," Tami said as she dabbed at her teary eyes.

"Of course we would welcome you. Not only because it would be what Mom wanted, but because you are our sister, and our blood," Blake said. He pulled Tami into his arms. "Welcome home, little sister. We know that you've a life and parents who have loved and raised you. Even so, you need to know this too will always be your home and we, your family."

Mrs. Darnell stood silently dabbing at her wet eyes with her lace handkerchief and watching all her grandchildren. She turned to River and hugged her.

"Thank you, River, for not giving up, for seeing this through to the end. You've righted a wrong that happened over twenty years ago. You've given me the one thing I believed would never come to fruition. For that, you have my eternal gratitude," she whispered. She pulled away and smiled at her. "I feel I've gained another granddaughter in you and I expect that you and your beau will visit me often."

"Oh, no…we're not," River stammered.

"Give it time, child." Mrs. Darnell smiled and her face lit up. She turned and winked at Gage.

"Let's take Tami up to the house," Garnet said. She reached out and took Tami's hand in hers and offered her other hand to her grandmother.

The quartet started for the house. Suddenly, Blake turned back and walked over to River.

"I can't even begin to say thank you."

"You just did. Go be with your family. You know where to find me, when you're ready."

Six weeks later…

A KEY RATTLED in River's apartment door. She ran

over to open it. Gage stood there juggling take-out from one of their favorite places and a wrapped box. She kissed him and took the gift from his hand.

River couldn't put her finger on the exact time Gage managed to slip under her guard. All she knew for sure was he had. And, each day that followed, she'd grown more in love with him. She didn't know what the future held. She realized he could still break her heart. Right now—she didn't care. She promised herself, to live in the moment and soak up every drop of happiness.

"For me?" she asked shaking the wrapped box.

"Naturally." He set the boxes on the kitchen table and picked up a glass of wine from the counter. "Don't you think we should talk about finding a bigger place? I mean, I'm here nearly all the time. I want to make it official."

"I don't want to leave my girlfriends. However, I did speak to Uncle Mike today. He said the unit at the end of the hall will be empty in another month. The apartment has two bedrooms, a large living area, and a kitchen and dining room."

She opened the box and found a stunning cobalt

blue charmeuse pullover. "It's perfect, I love it!"

"I thought it would highlight your sparkling eyes."

Music from River's favorite oldies station streamed through the speakers. A Beatles song started playing. Gage grabbed River and started dancing to the song, *P.S. I love you.* As the song reached the chorus, he belted out his own lyrics: "P.I.—I Love You."

River froze and stared at him.

He continued singing…*"you, you, you…I love you."*

She jumped into his arms, wrapped her legs around his waist, and kissed him, over and over, until he could hardly breathe.

"I don't know a fancy song. I can tell you, though, I do love you, more than I ever thought possible," she whispered between breaths.

"That's music to my ears." It was that precise moment Gage knew he could never get enough of River Nightingale.

About The Author

Joanne writes romantic suspense, paranormal, and supernatural. A transplant from upstate New York, Joanne lives with her husband and Doberman, in their home located on the Olympic Peninsula with a panoramic view of the Olympic Mountains.

When she's not writing, she loves to travel and enjoys time with her family and friends. In her prior life, Joanne showed dogs, worked in personnel, and managed her husband's forensic engineering firm.

Joanne is a PAN member of Romance Writers of America, Kiss of Death, Greater Seattle Romance Writers Chapter, Sisters In Crime, and Fantasy, Futuristic & Paranormal. She served as President of Peninsula Romance Writers, which was Debbie Macomber's home chapter.

Other Books by Joanne Jaytanie

Miss Demeanor, P.I.
Twice As Bad, Book 2

Hunters & Seekers
Salvaging Truth, Book 1

The Winters Sisters
Chasing Victory, Book One
Payton's Pursuit, Book Two
Willow's Discovery, Book Three
Corralling Kenzie, Book Four

Forever Christmas In Glenville
Christmas Reflections
Christmas Ivy

Love, Take Two
Love's Always Paws-Able
Building Up to Love
Uncharted Love

Made in the USA
Coppell, TX
24 January 2024

28134322R10081